D1447782

Whynk

Dedication

To the women in my genetic line who I have had the honor
and privilege of knowing, loving, learning from, and teaching:
Enola Dumas Narcisse (grandmother), Earline Sarah Narcisse Borne
(mother), and Leah Pierre (daughter). Thank you for your
abilities to nurture, teach, and learn.

You are the ones who combed our hair daily so that we would
be presented well in our communities.
You represent all mothers who by
example and instruction allow us to hone skills
so our children would receive the untold accolades
of children who were well groomed.

To my daughter, Leah, who sat quietly and patiently
or noisily and fidgety as I combed her hair.

And to myself, for the patience and diligence I developed
during this daily task. We all did this so that the women
of our future would benefit.

—D. H. Whyatt

Written by D. H. Whyatt
Illustrated by Corey Wolfe and Carlos Valenti
Designed by Willabel Tong, Art Director

Library of Congress Control Number: 2020924918

ISBN: 978-1-7358547-0-0

Published by Whynk Publishing.
For more information, please contact us: info@whynkpublishing.com

For more about the artists, please visit:
Corey Wolfe ~ coreywolfe.com
Carlos Valenti ~ carlosvalenti.blogspot.com

Consultants:
Lisa Rojany ~ editorialservicesofla.com
Peter Bowerman ~ wellfedwriter.com

Miranda's Green Hair

by D. H. Whyatt

ILLUSTRATIONS BY

Corey Wolfe AND Carlos Valenti

AND DESIGN BY WILLABEL TONG

Miranda just loved to jump up and down,
to run up a hill and then roll back down.
But there is one thing she hated,
despised it for sure,
and today was the day for that terrible chore.

"Miranda, Miranda, come in here, my dear.
We're visiting Grandma. There's nothing to fear.
I must wash your hair. I must do it now.
Imagine how gorgeous. Imagine it! Wow!"

"I'll wash it, condition it,
and comb it up nice.
Remove all the dirt
and style it just right.
And when you're all ready,
all cleaned up and dressed,
Grandma will see you
at your very best."

3

"I DON'T want to wash it.
I just want to play.
You know Grandma loves
my green hair this way."

Miranda ran off,
and what did Mom see?
Miranda was rolling in
leaves under a tree.

"Miranda, Miranda, your hair is a mess.
It's worse than ever, you have to confess.
It's full of dirt, grass, and weeds,
and if you look closely, there are even some seeds."

"Miranda!"

Miranda ran up the hill and rolled down once more.
Her mom shook her head and yelled through the door:
"Miranda!"

Miranda ran to the porch
and then through the door.
She was running so fast,
she tripped on the floor.

She got up and covered her hair with her hands.
She wanted nothing to do with mom's hair combing plans.

"Grandma won't care if
my hair is not clean.
We don't have to wash it.
You're just being MEAN."

"As I told you before,
your hair looks a disaster!
It's like being in a circus,
and I'm the ringmaster.
I must wash your hair now.
I must wash it today.
I can't have your grandma
see you looking this way."

"Not today,
not tomorrow.
I'll never do it.
I WON'T let you
touch it or try to
comb through it."

Miranda ran up the stairs.

She ran
down
the hall.

She hid in her closet
under toys,
skirts, and
dolls.

"Miranda, Miranda, I know you're up here.
I'll find you. I will. I know that you're near!"
Mom looked in the bathroom and under the bed.
But she couldn't find Miranda or her little green head.

"You'll have to come down.
You'll have to come soon.
You'll get hungry for sure.
I'll find you by noon."

Miranda, Miranda, quiet as a mouse,
came out of the closet and sneaked out of the house.

She ran to the woods and skipped through the trees.
Her green hair was flying all free in the breeze.
She'd done it! It was over. She'd left it behind.
No hair washing for her. No hair washing this time.

She splashed in a stream
and napped under a tree.
But now it was noon,
and she was getting hungry.
She sighed, then she cried…

"Oh, what have I done?
I'm tired, and I'm starving.
I shouldn't have run."

The tree looked at Miranda
and decided to speak.
As she stretched forth her
branches they started to creak.
The tree said, "Miranda,
look up here, my dear."
Then touched her small
shoulder, asking,
"Why are you here?"

"I ran from my home.
I ran from my bed.
Mom wants to wash my hair,
but it hurts my whole head.
I ran away fast, without any food.
And now my stomach doesn't feel very good."

15

The tree thought about the little girl's state
and decided that some of her fruit would taste great.

So down
dropped an apple,
red and delicious,
crunchy and sweet,
and oh-so-nutritious.

16

The tree thought about the night soon to fall.
She thought about Miranda, green hair and all.
When it turns dark (when all's not what it seems),
she imagined Miranda and all of her screams.

The tree tucked its roots deep down in the ground,
and talked to the other trees all around.
"There is a girl named Miranda hiding out here.
If you see her nearby don't give her a scare.
Keep her safe. Keep her warm. Keep her in sight.
We'll help her get home while there's still light."

In the kitchen at home, Miranda's mom cried,
"I've looked everywhere. Where does that child hide?
Miranda, Miranda, where could you be?
If you'll come out of hiding, I'll let your hair be."
Mom called on the phone to all of their friends.
And neighbors came by to help look once again.

She paced back and forth.
She just couldn't sit down.
Miranda was nowhere in
the house to be found.

The trees kept their vigil, and they watched her all day.
She was like a small puppy that had just run away.
She wasn't as scared as they thought she should be,
not even when she fell down and scraped up her knee.

Then all of a sudden Miranda's hair gave her a fright.
She pulled and she tugged with all of her might.
But her wavy, green hair was caught in the bushes.
She couldn't get free, not even with pushes.

The hair got more tangled as she put up a fight.
The trees wanted to laugh it was such a sight.
"Miranda, Miranda, stop thrashing about.
The twigs will then loosen, and you can get out."

Miranda calmed down
and gave some small pushes.
The hair slowly untangled
and got free of the bushes.

"That's what it feels like
when Mom combs my hair.
She pulls and she tugs,
and it hurts everywhere.
The teeth of the comb
get stuck in the strands.
And that dumb brush hurts
no matter where it lands.
So I won't let her wash it.
I won't, I don't dare.
I hate it when Mom
washes my hair!"

"Miranda, my dear,
what will you do?
Your mom is just trying
to make your hair look
brand new."

"It hurts me me so badly, I won't have it combed. As long as it hurts, I WON'T go back home."

Said the barn owl
to the trees down below,
"This is not a great place
for a little girl, you know."

So the trees held
a meeting to come
up with a plan.
The animals all came to
lend them a hand.
"She must go back home.
She must go back soon.
Her mom must be worried,
she left home before noon."

They argued back and forth
about what should be done.
To hear them all yapping
was really quite fun.
The birds chirped.
The squirrels chuckled.
The owls had their say.
They created a plan to help
Miranda that day.

26

"Miranda, my dear, there's a way it won't hurt.
We'll wash your green hair. We'll get rid of the dirt."
The eagle spotted some rocks leading into
a stream. They'd use this
small pool to get that
hair clean.

Miranda agreed
to give it a try.
So she went to the rock
at the water nearby.

28

The crane held her closely so she wouldn't fall in.
Then a trusting Miranda leaned back with a grin.
She dipped and she dipped, but it wouldn't come clean.
Something was wrong. The hair was dull green.

The owl gave a hoot to the eagle in flight,
"We need some shampoo. Her hair looks a fright."
So the squirrels borrowed shampoo
from a camper nearby,
then tossed up
the tube when
the eagle flew by.

The eagle swooped down, handed it off to the crow, who dropped a big squirt onto her green hair below. Her new outdoor friends were so loving and kind. They washed it. They rinsed it. They cleaned it real fine. And when they were done, when the washing was through,

Miranda's wavy green hair shimmered like new.

31

The crane was up next, with his long pointy beak,
and he parted the hair with one lightning quick streak.
The crane held her head steady and did it twice more.
And when he was done it was parted in four.

"Miranda, my dear,
are you doing okay?"

"Yes, I'm fine.
It doesn't hurt
much this way."

Four little blue birds held each section at bay.
They didn't want all that hair in the way!
Their plan was to detangle from bottom to top,
for Miranda's green hair was as thick as a mop.

Miranda thought
about the comb,
and she started to cry.

34

So two little hummingbirds decided to give hair combing a try.
They used their small claws like a fine-tooth comb.
They may have been little, but they were really quite strong.

Though they fluttered and flapped with all of their might, that long curly hair put up a good fight.

So they swirled her green hair around and around until Miranda's green hair looked just like a crown.

They combed it, they twisted it. They thought it looked good.

But then came the wind, which did what it would.

The little birds stopped humming.
They looked really stressed.
Now Miranda's green hair looked just like a nest.

37

Said the eagle above to the crew down below: "I have something to tell you that you may not know. I've flown over the sky for many a mile. And no little girl gets her hair combed in that style."

They took a deep breath. They'd start over again,
so they unwrapped her hair from beginning to end.

Then the crane parted the hair in four like before.
And the crow took a turn to try combing it once more.
But it was taking so long, the hair started to dry.
"Oh, no!" said the crow, "Dry hair at this point
just won't comply."

As luck would have it, the wind blew a wave
that crashed onto a rock, creating a shower of water
dew drops.

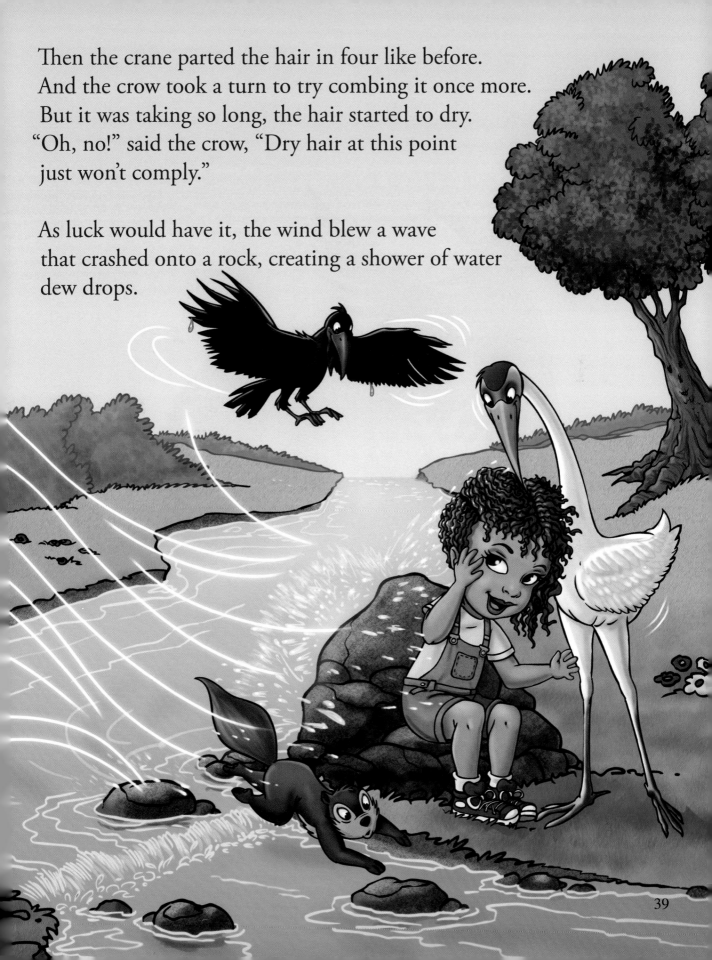

39

Now that her hair was wetted once more,
the crow finished combing the last lock of four.

They'd washed it!
Detangled it!
And parted it, too.
Now one last step
and they'd almost
be through.

With the wind picking up there was no time to spare.
It was time to start styling Miranda's green hair.
The crow combed through the hair
again and again, but the hair
wouldn't stay because of
the wind. Giving up now
would be a disaster. They needed
a good brush, and they needed
to work faster.

The squirrel knew her tail
was as soft as can be.
She wanted to help, so she
climbed down from the tree.

It was getting quite late, so they started to rush.
The squirrel used her tail like a soft bristle brush.
She brushed and she brushed, then she patted it twice.
But something was wrong, it just wouldn't stay nice.

Maybe some oil would help smooth out her hair. So the owl took off flying, and not far from there. A fat aloe vera plant bent in the breeze. She took it to Miranda and gave it a squeeze.

Then the crane parted an arc across the crown of her head.

Miranda's little face started turning bright red.
The crow gathered the hair and pulled it up high.
He began to twist, and Miranda started to cry.

The crane thought, *This is really not great.*

They all started talking. They were not yet through.
They looked at each other. "What will we do?"
Let's give her a break, and we'll think for a while."
At the word *break* Miranda broke into a smile.

Miranda ran and she jumped and she looked at the sky.
She skipped and she sang as the time just passed by.

"I can't wait to finish.
I can't wait to see.
I'm coming to sit
back under the tree."

Miranda's excitement encouraged them all.
They'd finish her hair just before nightfall.

The crow called together
the rest of the group.
"Okay guys, this here's
the scoop.
We'll bind it and braid it
and tuck all the strays.
There's no other way to
make her hair stay."

The honeysuckle vine did the binding just right.
The hair wasn't too loose, and it wasn't too tight.
And when they were done, the hair it behaved.
It stayed in one place when the wind blew a wave.

48

Now that the binding
was finally done,
two little blue birds twisted
her hair into a bun.

Then three little
hummingbirds braided
the rest just for fun.

They braided
her hair with
flowers in rows.
The braids were
so long, they
reached down
to her toes.

Two butterflies landed
on top like some bows.
And dragonflies held
the braids neatly in rows.

The animals marveled
at what they did see.
Miranda looked like
a princess under that tree!

"Miranda, Miranda,
your hair is beautiful now.
We've washed it,
and combed it.
Your hair looks like…
wow!"

"I wish I could look.
I wish I could see.
What do I look like?
Do I look pretty?"

The owl hooted loudly,
"You look like a dream!
Just walk over there and
look in the stream."

When she saw her reflection, she had to look twice.

"You washed it. You combed it.
You fixed it up nice."

"Usually I hate this,
you know that I do.
But this wasn't so bad!
And it's all thanks
to you."

"Miranda, my dear, now that you're calm.
It's definitely time to go home to your mom."

53

The birds gave a whistle, and who should come running—
but a black and white horse, whose long mane was quite stunning.

Miranda jumped on the back of the beautiful horse
that galloped so fast, so fine with such force.

They looked at the lights
at her farm house below.
And the horse took off running,
and none too slow.

56

They were going so fast she thought they might crash,
but he got her home safely, quick as a flash.

"Who did this? I'm serious. Who combed your green hair? Who fixed it so pretty and with so much care?"

"Miranda, Miranda, where have you been?
I looked everywhere. I called all our friends."

Then her mother just stopped
and stared for a while.
And all of a sudden
she started to smile.

"My friends in the woods! It took them awhile.
And then when I saw it, it just made me smile!"

Miranda thought to herself as she drifted to sleep,

"If you're the owner of frizzy green hair,
please tell your mom to handle with care.
It doesn't take much to be ever so brave,
when someone knows how to make green hair behave."

The
End

Although D. H. Whyatt extols the virtue of having a well-groomed head of hair, on this day over six decades ago (which was probably her photographic debut), her own soft curly brown hair had not yet met with the small baby-comb, the baby-soft brush, or a ribbon to bind it.

Thank You

To God, my Creator and Father, ever present through every step of the process and responsive to every request or cry for help no matter how big or small.

Family and Friends

To my husband, Jeffery, for his support as I worked my way through this long process. To my daughter and friend, Leah, who was instrumental in making sure that Miranda's journey made sense every step of the way. To my son, Evyn, whose insight and perception I am very grateful for; who on one day of great discouragement, fear, and apprehension, put things into perspective. He said "Mom, what is the worst thing that can possibly happen? If you don't sell even one book, your grandchildren will have one of the cutest, most expensive children's books ever produced." That made me smile.

To my brother and sisters whom I love dearly and am so grateful for all of their support and encouragement (Charley, Coleen, Carla, and Avis). To my good friend Dr. Marva Lewis who was instrumental and supportive throughout the development of this book.

And thank you to Ms. Prue Bostwick, a very kind, generous artist from Australia, whom I met in Papua New Guinea. She selflessly gave of her time to help with book design and development in the early stages of this wonderful journey.

The Team

Good writing is one thing, being able to make something that has never before existed come alive visually is in a whole different league. I wrote and rewrote, and put my writing forward for critique and correction until it was complete. And to play here, one must have a good team. I have been blessed with a great team.

When it comes to thanks, the line is long. As with any other major production, the talented people needed to complete the project are many. The quality of book that is *Miranda's Green Hair* would not be available to you if it were not for the talent and hard work and commitment of the following people:

Author's Assistant: Leah Pierre—who identified conflicts, recommended changes, and added touches so that the process kept moving forward in an orderly and meaningful manner.

Editor: Lisa Rojany—who made sure that *Miranda* made a respectable debut into the world of children's literature.

Business Consultant: Peter Bowerman—whose book *The Well-Fed Self Publisher*, freed me to write untethered from the fear of never being published.

With a Special Thank You to Miranda's Core Team of Professionals

Because of you, Miranda has a well-deserved place alongside all of the other wonderful children's books....

Illustrator: Carlos Valenti—who was able to translate written words from a visual concept I could see only in my mind's eye, into illustrations that are even more delightful than I could have ever imagined and gave life to Miranda.

Illustrator: Corey Wolfe—whose imagination brought color to Miranda's world with such vibrancy and detail that it still takes my breath away, and I hope it does the same for you and your little one every time you read it.

Art Director and Children's Book Designer: Willabel Tong—whose input in emails, texts, and phone calls number in the thousands. Her collaborative spirit, eye for detail, and ability to craft how the story and art would unfold, from the beginning page to the end of this journey, is what allows *Miranda's Green Hair* to stand proudly among other books written for children.

To my team, my family and my friends, you have my heartfelt gratitude.

—D. H. Whyatt